PATRICIA SCANLAN

FAIR-WEATHER FRIEND

Patricia Scanlan is the author of ten Number One best-selling novels, *City Girl*, *City Lives*, *City Woman*, *Apartment 3B*, *Finishing Touches*, *Foreign Affairs*, *Mirror Mirror*, *Promises Promises*, *Francesca's Party* and *Two for Joy*. Her first adult literacy book, *Second Chance*, was published in 1997 and her second, *Ripples*, in 1999. She lives in Dublin.

All royalties from the Irish sales of the Open Door series go to a charity of the author's choice. *Fair-Weather Friend* royalties go to Irish Guide Dogs for the Blind, Cork.

NEW ISLAND *Open Door*

FAIR-WEATHER FRIEND
This version first published in Ireland in 2004
by New Island
2 Brookside
Dundrum Road
Dublin 14

www.newisland.ie

A CIP catalogue record for this book is available from the British Library

ISBN 1 904301 47 9

New Island receives financial assistance from
The Arts Council (An Chomhairle Ealaíon), Dublin, Ireland.

Typeset by New Island
Printed in Ireland by ColourBooks.
Cover design by Artmark

3 5 4 2

Dear Reader,

On behalf of myself and the other contributing authors, I would like to welcome you to the fourth Open Door series. We hope that you enjoy the books and that reading becomes a lasting pleasure in your life.

Warmest wishes,

Patricia Scanlan.

Patricia Scanlan
Series Editor

THE OPEN DOOR SERIES IS DEVELOPED WITH THE ASSISTANCE OF THE CITY OF DUBLIN VOCATIONAL EDUCATION COMMITTEE.

Chapter One

'Why do you bother going on holidays with Melissa Harris? She's such a cow. She only uses you, you know,' Denise Mason said crossly. She ate some chicken korma and took a sip of white wine.

Sophie glared at her sister. 'She's not *that* bad!' she snapped. She dipped a piece of naan bread into her tikka sauce. She was annoyed and did not try to hide it.

'Oh come on, Sophie, she's a walking cow. She always has been. She drops you like a hot potato as soon as there's a bloke on the scene. Then you don't see her for dust until she's been dumped. When she needs a shoulder to cry on she's back in double-quick time.'

Sophie made a face. 'Stop giving out.'

'I'm not giving out,' Denise said. 'I'm just telling you things for your own good. You're too soft with her. You always have been. It's time you told her where to get off.

'Remember last year? You were supposed to go on holidays with her. She dropped you at the last minute because she met Mister Wonderful. She took off to Spain with him. What kind of a so-called friend is that?' Denise pronged a stuffed mushroom and ate it with relish.

Sophie looked at her younger sister with envy. Denise could eat and drink all round her. She never put on an ounce. Sophie would be up two pounds at least on the scales after this pig-out.

'What happened to Mister Wonderful anyway?' Denise topped up their wineglasses. 'I thought they were going back to Spain this year.'

'She found out that he was two-timing her. She's in bits. Really she is, Denise. I've never seen her this bad,' Sophie said earnestly. 'She was crazy about Tony. Nuts about him. He was the love of her life.'

'Don't be daft, Sophie!' Denise scoffed. 'How could *he* be the love of her life? She's so much in love with herself, there's no room for anyone else.'

'Oh leave her alone,' Sophie muttered.

'Well *I* would have told her where to get off if she had asked me to go on holidays with only a week's notice. I would have said no,' Denise retorted, helping herself to some of the aloo saag. 'She's using you. Can't you see that?'

It's all right for you, Sophie thought glumly. She studied her bright-eyed, well-groomed, very confident younger sister. Denise had friends to beat the band. Men fell over themselves trying to get a date with her. She breezed through life with not a care in the world. She was very much the woman about town. She worked in the PR department of a large publishing company. At the age of twenty-two, Denise drove her own company car.

Sophie was two years older. She drove an old Fiesta that she'd had for the last four years. She was a children's nurse. While she enjoyed her job, she felt that her life lacked the glamour and excitement of her sister's.

Her two closest friends had got

married within six months of each other. In the last two years she'd had no one to go on holidays with. The idea of going on a singles holiday filled her with dread. So she had taken up the offer of two weeks in Majorca with Melissa Harris – much to her sister's annoyance.

Sophie sighed and took a slug of her Australian wine. The Indian meal she'd been looking forward to with Denise was turning into a lecture. The only fights she ever had with Denise were over Melissa Harris. Denise and Melissa had never got on. They never would. It made life very difficult sometimes – like right now. She drank some more wine while Denise kept on and on about what a user Melissa was. She remembered something her father used to say when she was small: 'The truth always hurts.' She didn't like when Denise called Melissa a user. Because if Melissa was a user, Sophie was the one being used. And no one liked to feel they were being used.

Chapter Two

She'd known Melissa since her schooldays: blonde, blue-eyed, bubbly and very, very selfish.

Melissa was the centre of the universe in her own eyes. Or, as Denise cruelly called her, the Queen of the Me, Me, Me Planet. She was an only child, spoilt by doting parents. Melissa swanned through life taking adoration as her due.

In Sophie, she had the perfect handmaiden. It had been so from that first moment in the playground when Melissa had decided that she preferred

Sophie's little black-velvet bow to the red ribbon that held her own golden pony-tail.

Sophie had handed over the bow without a peep. She was spellbound by Melissa's baby-blue eyes. Eyes that had the most perfect long black lashes. The invitation to join Melissa's gang filled her with joy. The entire class longed to be a member of Melissa's gang. Only the chosen few were given the honour. And the honour was withdrawn regularly, depending on Melissa's mood and whim. Sophie would often find herself on the outside of the golden circle until Melissa had need of her services again.

This was the pattern of their friendship, through childhood, through their teens and while Melissa studied to become a beauty consultant and Sophie was a student nurse. Weeks could go by and Sophie wouldn't hear a peep from Melissa. Then some crisis would occur. Melissa would arrive at Sophie and Denise's flat in search of tender loving care and sympathy. She would sob over her latest heartbreak and declare 'All Men Are Bastards.'

Tony Jenkins was the most recent addition to the All Men Are Bastard's list. He and Melissa had been about to take Spain by storm. Sadly, Melissa had discovered him in a steamy clinch with a work-mate at a friend's engagement party. It seemed they were having a rip-roaring affair. Before she left the party, she had thrown red wine over her rival's brand-new white Versace halter-neck. It had been a very gratifying moment she told Sophie. Then she burst into tears.

'I really loved him.' Melissa wept. 'I just don't understand what he sees in her, Sophie. She's an awful airhead and she's got a flabby bum! When I think of all the times I did work on her hairy lip. I should have let the needle slip and scarred the sly cow for life.'

Sophie made a mental note *never* to let Melissa do work on her. Not that Melissa ever did beauty treatments for her now that she was qualified. It had been a different kettle of fish when she'd been training and needed guinea-pigs. Sophie had been manicured, pedicured and french polished. She had been tweezed and waxed within an inch of her life. *That* had been painful! Sophie had never waxed her legs again after what she had gone through with Melissa. The pain when Melissa had pulled off the strips had brought tears to her eyes.

'Sissy,' Melissa had jeered. Sophie had been raging. Her friend was so ungrateful. She took so much for granted. But mad as she was with Melissa, she was madder at herself for being such a doormat. Would she never learn?

When Melissa had asked her to let her practise waxing again before her finals, Sophie had told her to get lost. It was one of the few times she didn't give in to her friend's pleadings. There had been a frosty silence for weeks. Then Melissa had found out that the hairdresser she thought she had fallen in love with was gay. That had been a mega trauma. There had been weeks of sobbing on Sophie's shoulder about her heart being truly broken.

'I'll never fall in love again,' Melissa had stated dramatically. Then she had met Tony Jenkins and fallen hook, line and sinker. She'd even sunk to a new low in their friendship. She'd ditched

Sophie to go on holidays with her new boyfriend. Denise had been hopping mad when she heard the news. 'Don't you dare *ever* speak to that bitch again. If I get my hands on her I'll murder her,' she yelled. Sophie didn't know which was worse, Denise's rantings or Melissa's betrayal.

Sophie hadn't spoken to Melissa for months. It was the longest they hadn't spoken. Then Christmas had come and her soft heart got the better of her when Melissa sent her a Christmas card.

Now that the divine Tony had done the dirty on Melissa, she had come running to Sophie for comfort. This new disaster was the trauma of traumas, Sophie decided as she watched her friend pace the room.

'That tart is going to Spain with him. Can you *believe* it?' Melissa was bursting with rage. Her flawless pale skin was red with temper. 'Sophie, you simply have to come on holidays with me. I'm damned if flabby-bum Jane is going to come into the salon sporting a tan and showing off photos of her and The Rat.

'We'll go somewhere and get the best tan ever and find the most gorgeous hunks to take care of us. Our photos will make that rat pea-green with envy. I'll make sure he gets to see them. But even if he comes crawling back on his hands and knees, he's history, Sophie. I'll go straight to the travel agent tomorrow and book a holiday for us.'

Melissa of course assumed that Sophie would drop everything and be thrilled to go on holidays with her.

'I don't know. It's very short notice. I wasn't planning to go abroad,' Sophie protested. 'I'm a bit strapped for cash.'

'Don't be silly, Sophie. What do you mean short notice? You're not *doing* anything are you? You weren't planning on going away were you?' Melissa demanded. 'I'm broke too. When I found out about The Rat and that two-faced so-called friend, I went out and blew a fortune on a little black dress. It's to die for, Sophie, but my Visa card is having a nervous breakdown. It will have to be a cheap holiday for me too. But who cares? You and I will strut our stuff on the beach and we won't have to spend a penny,' Melissa said confidently. Her eyes were shining at the thought of her next conquest. She couldn't wait to let Tony Jenkins see that he wasn't the only man in the universe.

A fortnight in the sun would be nice, Sophie thought dreamily. Lazing on a lounger with a big, fat blockbuster novel and an ice-cold beer or a glass of chilled wine. Melissa could strut her perfectly toned and sculptured stuff. Sophie would be quite content to lie on her lounger, her flabby bits not being at all suitable for strutting.

Chapter Three

Two weeks later they were sitting in a bar at the airport. They were waiting to board a TransAer flight to Majorca. They had been delayed for three hours. Melissa was fit to be tied.

"This is bloody daft. The plane hasn't even left Palma yet. We're going to be here for *hours*! That's a whole day wasted. It will be the middle of the night before we get to … Portal … Portal … wherever that place we're going to is.'

'Portal Nous,' Sophie murmured.

'I hope it's going to be a bit lively. It's three miles from Palma Nova. It was all I could get at such short notice,' Melissa fretted.

'It will be fine, Melissa, stop panicking,' Sophie said, trying not to loose her cool. 'Now let's have coffee and a sandwich. I'm a bit peckish.'

Her nerves were frayed. Melissa had whined and moaned non-stop about their delayed flight. Then she'd started on about the awful betrayal she had suffered at the hands of The Rat. It was doing Sophie's head in.

'Oh no, not coffee! Let's go and get pissed.' Melissa flung back her golden hair and stood up from the hard chair she'd been sitting on. She was quite aware that every male eye in the lounge was upon her. She swanned towards the bar in her skin-tight white jeans and tightly fitting black halter-neck.

Sophie's heart sank. If Melissa went on the sauce she was in for a hard time. Melissa, unfortunately, could not drink. She always needed looking after when she was the worse for wear. Many were the times Sophie had hauled Melissa into loos or shoved her head out of taxi windows as she threw up all round her. If she started drinking with hours to go before their flight it would be a disaster.

'Now Melissa go easy. You've already had three tequila slammers,' she warned.

'Oh stop it, Sophie. You're not my mother!' Melissa snapped as she ordered another drink. 'Do you want one?' she asked crossly.

'OK, I'll have a Bud,' Sophie agreed. It might shut Melissa up for a while. She'd be happy enough to sit in the boarding area and read one of the six books she had brought with her. She couldn't decide which to start with. The second *Bridget Jones* or the latest John Grisham thriller. She was so looking forward to getting into them. Sophie liked reading. She liked being taken into another world. She liked getting away from her own boring life for a while. Melissa thought reading was a waste of time.

Three hours later, Melissa was well and truly plastered. She had puked twice. Now she was draped across a tall, dark, arty type who was waiting on a flight to Greece.

'We should change our flight and go to Greece ...' she slurred gaily.

'Off you go,' muttered Sophie. She was very pissed off.

Two hours after that they finally boarded their flight. Melissa promptly fell asleep. She snored loudly for the duration, her head resting on Sophie's shoulder. Sophie couldn't believe her luck. She pulled *Bridget Jones* out of her travel bag and laughed her way across France and Spain. Beside her Melissa's musical snores drowned out the roar of the jet engines.

Unfortunately, a bumpy descent into Palma airport disturbed both Melissa and her stomach. For the third time that day, Sophie resisted the urge to drown her in a toilet bowl.

It took another hour to collect their luggage. Then they had to find the coach that was to bring them to their apartment. Sophie found it hard to keep her eyes open as the air-conditioned coach finally sped along the motorway towards their destination. She half-listened to the rep as she reminded her clients to use lots of sun factor protection. Grinning, the rep also warned them not to drink too much San Miguel.

Melissa was green-faced. She groaned at the thought of beer. She promised herself she was never going to drink again. Once again she fell asleep. Her snores rippled around the bus. Sophie tried to pretend that she didn't know her. She stared out into the darkness and was sorry she had come.

Chapter Four

By the time the coach pulled into the small two-storey apartment block, Sophie was wrecked. It didn't look ultra-modern she noted as they stopped outside a tatty-looking building. It had white, flaking paint and two pots of dried-out, wilting flowers at the entrance. The tiles were cracked and grubby.

She was too tired to care as a sullen receptionist took their passports and handed her the key to room 103. They were the only passengers to get off the coach so at least the check-in was quick. Sophie yawned wearily as they click-clacked their way down a brown tiled floor, dragging their luggage behind them.

'It's a bit kippy,' Melissa moaned as Sophie struggled to get the big black key to turn in the lock.

Basic was how Sophie would have described it. She switched on the light to see a white-painted room, furnished with a shabby sofa and two chairs with cigarette burns on the arms. A pine table and four chairs stood opposite the French doors. A small kitchen had a two-ring cooker, sink and noisy fridge.

The bedroom had a built-in wardrobe whose doors didn't close properly. There were two beds, each with a small bedside locker. The bathroom, decorated in mustard-coloured tiles, was not a place she'd spend too long in, she decided. It was three in the morning. She was exhausted. Melissa's shrieks of dismay were the last thing she needed.

'Let's go to bed. You chose the apartment, Melissa. It's not my fault. I've had a long day. I don't want to hear any more about it. I've had enough, so zip it,' she exploded as she pulled off her T-shirt and jeans and dived into the nearest bed.

'There's no need to be like that,' Melissa sniffed huffily as she undressed. 'Can I have some of your bottled water to wash my teeth? My mouth tastes horrible.' Melissa of course would never be so organised as to have bottled water. That's what Sophies were for.

'Help yourself.' Sophie yawned as she pulled the white sheet over her and buried her head under the long, thin pillow on the narrow bed. At least the sheets were crisp and clean, she thought drowsily. Minutes later she was fast asleep.

She awoke, she had no idea how much later, to high-pitched screeches coming from a frantic Melissa in the other bed.

'Get away from me! Get away from me!'

Dazed, Sophie sat up trying to remember where she was. Melissa was yelling like a madwoman. Her arms and legs were flailing in the dark. The unmistakable *buzzzzz* of a mosquito gave a clue to the cause of the drama.

'Oh for God's sake, Melissa, it's a mosquito. Spray some stuff on yourself and go to sleep,' she raged, finding the light and snapping it on.

'I think it's a bat!' wailed Melissa.

'It's *not* a bat. It's a mosquito. Here.'

She sprayed mosquito repellent over the tormented Melissa. She sprayed herself just in case and switched off the light.

'You've got really grumpy these days. You used to be much nicer,' Melissa said in her little-girl voice.

Spears of guilt prodded Sophie. She was being a bit of a bitch. Melissa had a fear of insects. 'Sorry!' she apologised. 'PMT,' she fibbed.

'We're going to have a good holiday, aren't we?' Melissa asked anxiously.

'We're going to have a *great* holiday. You're going to get a MEGA tan and find a hunk for your photos and The Rat is going to be the sorriest rat in the world.' Sophie was doing her best to be kind.

'Yes. He is a rat, isn't he? But I'm not taking him back. Definitely not.'

'No you're not. He's not worthy of you. There's a much nicer man waiting for you out there,' Sophie said kindly.

'Yes there is. A millionaire, possibly,' Melissa agreed. She always thought big. 'There's a marina around here somewhere where the jet set of the Mediterranean park their yachts.'

'Berth,' Sophie corrected, sleepily.

'What?'

'Berth their yachts, not park,' Sophie explained.

'Oh! Right, I better remember that.' She leaned on her elbow and stared over at Sophie. 'You know Majorca is very "in". Don't forget Princess Di used to come here. The Spanish royal family come here and Michael Douglas brought Catherine Zeta-Jones here. He has a big villa in Deya. I've read about it in *Hello!* Maybe we should go there for a day. We'll hire a car.'

'Fine,' murmured Sophie, wishing Melissa would go back asleep.

'Imagine if I met a millionaire! I

might even invite Tony and Jane to the wedding,' Melissa decided. 'That would really rub their noses in it. Wouldn't it, Sophie?'

Silence.

'Sophie?'

But Sophie was far away – in a deep and dreamless sleep.

She awoke to find sunlight dancing through the green shutters. Melissa was standing on the patio, arms crossed as she surveyed the scene in front of her.

'We can't possibly stay here, Sophie!' she declared, shocked. 'It's in the sticks. We don't even have a sea view. I definitely asked for a sea view. I was told I'd get one. The swimming-pool, if you could *call* it a swimming-pool, is no bigger than a *bath*!'

'Beggars can't be choosers, Melissa. After all it *was* a cancellation. We might not have got anywhere at such short notice.' Sophie scrambled out of bed and went to join her friend on the postage-stamp sized patio. The sun was shining. That was all that mattered in her opinion.

She gazed around at the dry, barren scrubland that backed onto a scree-filled cliff. A few pine trees grew here and there in little clumps. Their building was perched on a small hill. Below she could see other apartment blocks nestled among trees. In the distance was the glittering, silver-blue sparkle of sunlight dancing on water.

'There's your sea view,' she grinned, pointing. She stretched and breathed in the warm, scented Mediterranean breeze.

'This is the pits! The pits!' Melissa moaned. 'And look at those kids jumping up and down in the pool.

Horrible little beasties. Urrgh.' Melissa was not at all the maternal type.

'Well it did say suitable for families and it did say this was a quiet area in the brochure,' Sophie pointed out reasonably.

'I wonder would they move us to Palma Nova if I kicked up a fuss?' Melissa asked hopefully.

'Let's give it a chance for a day or two until we get our bearings. It's only ten minutes by taxi to Palma Nova anyway.'

'How do you know?' Melissa asked sulkily.

'The rep told us last night when you were asleep.'

'Oh, OK then. But if it's dead quiet we're moving and that's it,' Melissa declared as she marched back into the bedroom. 'Let's go and see what they serve for breakfast in that snack bar by the pool.'

'Yes, let's. I'm starving. And I'm dying for a cup of coffee. Let's explore.' Sophie didn't care if the apartment wasn't exactly the Ritz. She was in Majorca, the sun was shining and the beach beckoned.

They breakfasted on fresh coffee, croissants, crusty white rolls and jam and fruit. Even Melissa had to admit that it was tasty.

'Let's go to the marina and see if we can nab a millionaire,' she suggested gaily. Her humour was improving by the minute.

Sophie heaved a mental sigh of relief. Maybe they *were* going to have a great holiday after all.

Chapter Five

'*This* is where we're going to breakfast from now on,' Melissa announced joyfully an hour later. They were strolling along the sea front, which had plenty of places to eat. A fifteen-minute walk from their apartment block had brought them to a completely different world.

'*This* is where I was born to be.' Melissa was giddy with excitement.

Yachts filled with beautiful people bobbed up and down on the gentle waves. The chic designer boutiques oozed posh. There were no prices on display. It was that kind of place.

Melissa strode along in her tight white shorts and bikini top, black glasses hiding her eyes. She looked like a film star. Sophie, in her denim shorts and black T-shirt, felt lumpy and frumpy beside her

'Let's go to the beach. It's getting hot. I'd like to go for a swim,' she said.

'Don't be silly, Sophie. We have to do some serious strutting here!' Melissa smiled at a tanned gigolo-type in a cream Armani suit.

Gigolo smiled back.

'See,' Melissa whispered.

'Melissa, you can strut. I'm going to the beach over there and I'm flopping.'

Gigolo was leering at Melissa from head to toe.

'See you on the beach. I'll get a lounger for you,' Sophie offered.

'Fine,' Melissa said snootily. 'If you want to miss the chance of a lifetime to go and slob out on a lounger, do it! I'm staying here.'

'Have fun,' Sophie said dryly as Gigolo flashed a wide, toothy grin at Melissa.

Melissa smiled back and fluttered her eyelashes.

Sophie left her to it.

The beach was a golden crescent of paradise. Pines tree fringed the edge of the cliffs. White-crested whisps of waves lapped the shore. It was off the beaten track. It wasn't crowded like the big resort beaches with their rows of white loungers. This beach was a little jewel, dotted with coconut umbrellas and delightful green loungers that could be hired for the day.

A small island lay about a mile offshore. There were no motor boats or hang-gliders or pedalos in sight. It was a most peaceful place. Sophie chose two loungers. She laid her towel on one, stripped to her black M&S bikini, lay down, closed her eyes and breathed deeply. She was in heaven. It was too relaxing even to read. A balmy little breeze whispered around her. The sea murmured its soothing, rhythmic lullaby. Sophie fell asleep.

Melissa joined her several hours later. She was on a high.

'Remember that guy?' she asked excitedly. 'He asked me would I like coffee. His name is Paulo and he's *absolutely* loaded! He's staying on a yacht with friends. They're cruising around the islands for a month. Imagine! He asked me out to dinner tonight. What will I wear Sophie? It will have to be something very sophisticated. Do you think the little black silk dress I bought would be OK?'

'It will be fine,' Sophie said, trying to sound interested. Melissa hadn't wasted any time. It looked like Sophie would be eating alone tonight. Her heart sank. Just as well she had plenty of books to read.

'I better get some serious sunbathing done before tonight.' Melissa unhooked her bikini top and slathered on some sun-tan oil. 'Sophie, it's great that we came to this place. I'd never have met anybody like Paulo in Palma Nova. The marina here is mega posh.' She gave a huge smile as she slid elegantly onto her lounger. She stretched out and closed her eyes.

Sophie tried not to feel envious as she surveyed her friend. Melissa had everything: looks, fabulous figure, bubbly personality. No wonder she was never man-less for long. A deep sigh came up from her toes as she looked at her own tummy that was not flat and taut like Melissa's. Hers was curved and rounded with a little, soft, jelly sort of bulge, no matter how tight she held her muscles in. Her thighs were dimpled at the top – not like Melissa's firm, toned, satin-skinned ones. And there was no denying that she had thick ankles, Sophie thought glumly as she looked at Melissa's shapely turned ankles and perfectly painted toes.

She felt fed up … and hungry.

'Will we have some lunch?' she asked.

'Oh God no! I couldn't eat a thing. I'm so excited.' Melissa yawned. 'Besides, Paulo bought me a gorgeous cake with the coffee, earlier.'

'Well I've had nothing to eat since breakfast. I'll just go and get something myself.' Sophie pulled on her sundress, grabbed her bag and flounced off.

'Enjoy it,' Melissa called airily after her. She hadn't even noticed that Sophie was annoyed.

Bitch! thought Sophie, simmering with resentment. Denise was right. Melissa was so self-centred. She thought the world revolved around her. Barely their first day on holidays and Sophie would have to eat alone twice.

She climbed the curving wooden steps up the side of the cliff and tried not to pant. She was so unfit it was a disaster. Still there was nothing she could do about it now. She might as well treat herself to something tasty for lunch, she decided. Food was always a great comforter.

It was quite nice to sit at a shaded table outside the cliff-top restaurant. She tucked into deep-fried squid in batter, with a crispy, crunchy side salad, and sipped ice-cold San Miguel beer.

For a treat she had a banana split smothered in cream. A girl had to have something to cheer her up. It was clear that Melissa was doing her hot-potato act. Sophie should have known better than to go on holidays with her. Denise had been right to warn her off. It was her own fault for not listening. She sighed deeply. She was fed up being a doormat. She had two choices now. She could sit and mope and feel sorry for herself. Or she could make up her mind to enjoy herself.

Sophie ate a spoonful of banana dripping with honey and cream. A balmy breeze ruffled her hair. She could be stuck in hot, humid London. She knew where she preferred to be – even if she was on her own. Melissa could get lost, Sophie decided. She didn't need a fair-weather friend in her life. From now on, she was going to be very cool indeed to Miss Melissa Harris.

Chapter Six

It was her fifth day alone. She might as well have come on a singles holiday after all. Sophie gave a deep sigh as she lay on the lounger in her favourite spot on the beach. She was annoyed with herself. Why, after all her good intentions, was she letting Melissa still get to her? She had to admit that even she had been surprised at how much of a user Melissa was.

Her 'friend' had spent two days with Paulo after the first big dinner-date.

'You don't mind, sweetie? He's such a pet. You should hear the lovely things he says to me and he's *such* a gentleman. He's really smitten, Sophie,' Melissa twittered as she changed into yet another outfit for a shopping trip to Palma. Her new boyfriend wanted to show her the sights. She was preening in front of the mirror in a vivid pink mini-dress. Sophie couldn't help a pang of envy. Melissa looked a million dollars. Her tan was golden. Her skin was like satin. The dress clung to all the right curves. She looked like a model.

That night she arrived back at the apartment, eyes shining.

'You'll never guess, Sophie! Paulo has asked me to go to Marbella on the yacht. I'm so excited.'

'How long are you going for?' Sophie demanded. 'You came on holidays with *me*, you know!' She was furious. She just couldn't help it. Melissa was rubbing her nose in it.

'Don't be like that, Sophie,' Melissa muttered defensively. 'This is the chance of a lifetime. Paulo is just what I need after The Rat.'

'Look, Melissa, you asked me to come on holidays with you. So far we've had one breakfast together and I've been left on my own ever since. You're being really selfish and I don't think much of your behaviour,' Sophie exploded.

'No *you're* being selfish!' Melissa rounded on her. 'This could be the best thing that's ever happened to me. If you were truly my friend you wouldn't be so mean.' She took her case from the wardrobe and began to pack. Sophie felt like thumping her. How typical of Melissa to turn the argument to her advantage.

They didn't speak for the rest of the night. The following morning Sophie kept her head under the pillow until she heard Melissa leave the apartment, dragging her case behind her.

So much for the gentleman. He didn't even come to collect the cow, she thought grumpily as she heard the click-clack of Melissa's white high heels fade away.

Surprisingly, once her anger and resentment had lessened, Sophie had actually enjoyed herself. She spent her days on the beach, reading and swimming. She liked watching the confident, noisy young Spaniards that gathered after school. It was an entertainment in itself just to watch them flirt. The girls were always dressed in fabulous bikinis that showed off their sallow, supple figures to perfection. Sophie promised herself that one day she too would be a beach princess. To start, she decided to walk for an hour every day. She got into the habit of walking along the seashore in the morning and in the evening. She was sure she could feel her thighs toning already.

At night she took a taxi to Palma Nova to eat at one of the beach-side restaurants. After her meal she strolled around the shops before going home to sit on her patio with her book and an ice-cold beer. The days melted into one another. Sophie realised that being on holidays alone was not half as daunting as she'd imagined. It was a liberation of sorts to know that she was perfectly able to enjoy herself alone.

She was relaxing in the late-afternoon sun, reading her crime novel, when a child's loud scream rent the air. Sophie looked up to see a little Spanish girl howling in pain. Her elderly grandfather was doing his best to comfort her. She had seen them at the beach every afternoon and thought they were very sweet. The grandfather doted on the little girl. He spent hours building big sand-castles to entertain her.

Sophie jumped up and hurried over. 'Can I help? I'm a nurse,' she said.

'Oh, thank you very much. Maria has been stung.' The man spoke perfect English.

Sophie soothed the little girl. 'Could you get me some vinegar from the café and I'll remove the sting and put some cream on it?' she asked the grandfather. The man spoke in rapid Spanish to a young student nearby who raced off up the steps towards the café.

Sophie kept talking in a calm tone to the little girl. She stopped screaming but whimpered pitifully.

'There, there, Maria, you'll be fine,'

Sophie said gently. She wiped the little girl's tears and offered her a Polo mint. Maria took one shyly and stopped crying. The old man looked very relieved.

'Thank you, thank you,' he said, patting Sophie on the arm.

Maria cried again as Sophie dabbed on the vinegar and removed the sting. But once the balm of antiseptic cream had done its trick, she was soon playing again, the drama forgotten.

The grandfather was very grateful. 'My daughter is pregnant and Maria's nanny had to return to Madrid, as her mother is very ill. So I have been taking care of her in the afternoons,' he explained. 'I am Juan Santander.' He held out his hand.

'Sophie Mason,' Sophie said.

They chatted for a while. It was nice to have someone to talk to.

'Your friend has not come back?' Juan remarked. 'She was here with you just one day.'

How observant, Sophie thought.

'She went on a cruise to Marbella.'

'Did you not want to go?' Juan looked surprised.

'I wasn't asked.' Sophie laughed.

'I see.' His eyes were kind. 'You will be here tomorrow?'

'Yes.'

'We will see you then.' Juan gathered up his granddaughter's bits and bobs. 'Tomorrow.'

Sophie watched them climb the path to the top of the cliff. She was glad to have been of help. He was a nice man and the little girl was a pet.

The following afternoon Sophie smiled as she saw the pair make their way down the steps. Maria raced over to proudly show off her bandage.

Juan winked. 'For such an injury a bandage was necessary. May we join you?'

'Please do,' Sophie invited.

'I wonder would you consider something?' Juan asked. 'I told my daughter what had happened and that you were a nurse. I told her that your friend had left you alone. She thought that was not very nice.' The old man shook his head. 'Not nice at all.' He smiled at Sophie. His brown eyes were kind. Sophie warmed to him. He reminded her of her own grandfather.

'We wondered if you would like to come and stay with us for a few days in our villa up in the hills? We have a pool and lovely grounds. It is most comfortable. I'm sure you would like it. My daughter is looking for someone to mind Maria and the new baby for at least six months. Maybe you might be interested in the job? If you spent a few days with us you would know if it is something you might consider.'

Sophie's eyes widened. It sounded like a fantastic offer. Leave dreary, humid, stuffy-old London and spend six months in this paradise. It sounded like a dream.

To her amazement she heard herself say, 'I'd love to.'

Juan rubbed his hands. 'Excellent. Can you come today?' he asked eagerly.

Sophie laughed. 'It's a bit sudden.'

'Why wait?' the old man said matter-of-factly.

'You're right,' Sophie agreed happily. 'I'll just go up to the apartment and get my things.'

'We'll collect you. Just give me the address,' Juan offered. 'We will pick you up. Won't we Maria?' He spoke in Spanish to his little granddaughter.

'*Sí, sí.*' She hopped up and down with delight.

'See you in an hour then,' Juan said briskly.

Sophie couldn't believe how impulsive she was being. But this was a chance of a lifetime. She'd kick herself if she let it pass. Although she didn't realise it, Melissa had done her a huge favour leaving her on her own.

'Thanks, Melissa,' Sophie murmured twenty minutes later as she flung her clothes into her suitcase. Life had just started to get a whole lot better.

Chapter Seven

Sophie had just packed her books when the door of the apartment burst open. She almost jumped.

Melissa appeared, red-eyed and on crutches.

'Thank God I'm here. That pig was so cruel,' she raged. 'I broke my leg on the yacht in Marbella. It was a nightmare. I had to go to hospital. He wouldn't even stay with me.' She looked at Sophie forlornly. 'Can you believe it?'

Sophie shook her head. She couldn't

believe her bad luck. Another ten minutes and she would have been gone. Melissa plonked onto her bed and threw her crutches on the floor.

'And then do you know what the bastard said when I got back to the yacht?' she said. 'He had the nerve to suggest that I fly from Malaga to Palma so I wouldn't delay their departure for Tangiers.' Her lips tightened into a thin line. 'I told him only if he paid for my flight and taxis to and from the airport.'

'And did he?' Sophie asked faintly.

'No he didn't!' retorted Melissa indignantly. 'The skinflint. It was only when I threatened to sue that his friends started to panic. They chipped in €50 each for the taxis and he had to pay for the plane ticket. What a miser! He couldn't get rid of me quick enough. I even had to hang around the marina. They let me off and then they sailed away before my taxi arrived. Can you believe it?' Melissa burst into tears. 'My luggage is in reception. Can you collect it for me?' she sniffled.

'Sure.' Sophie's heart sank as she headed off to reception. Trust Melissa to do something dramatic like break her leg. She wasn't too surprised at Paulo's behaviour. She hadn't liked him at all. But of course all Melissa had seen was the expensive clothes and jewellery – and the smarmy charm. They were two shallow people who were well suited to each other, she thought glumly. She grabbed Melissa's case angrily. Typical. Melissa was only back five minutes and already Sophie was running after her like a little skivvy.

She saw a big silver BMW drive up to the entrance. It was Juan and Maria.

She couldn't really go with them now and leave Melissa alone.

She'd leave you.

The thought popped into her head.

Don't fool yourself that she wouldn't!

Sophie stood still. What kind of a fool was she? Melissa wouldn't think twice about putting herself first. It was a way of life with her. It was time Sophie did the same. For once in her life she was going to be number one. She wasn't going to be a doormat for Melissa for the rest of her life. She lugged her friend's case back to the apartment.

'Why is your bag packed? Where are you going?' Melissa demanded as Sophie hauled the case into the bedroom.

'To stay with friends,' she said cheerfully. She dumped Melissa's case on the bed.

'What friends? You don't have friends here,' Melissa snorted.

'Yes I do. Look out the window.' Sophie felt a flicker of annoyance. Did Melissa think she was the only one to make friends with people on holidays? Some friend smarmy Paulo had turned out to be. The Santanders would be far more genuine. She was sure of it.

'What do you want me to look at?' Melissa demanded crossly.

'See that silver car over at reception?'

Melissa's jaw dropped. 'Who are they?'

'My friends,' Sophie drawled. 'Sorry I can't stay and explain, Melissa. Have to go.'

'But you can't go!' Melissa was stunned. 'You can't leave me! My leg is broken. I'm on crutches. How will I manage?'

'You'll be fine, Melissa. We're on the

ground floor. You can eat by the pool. You can sunbathe. What more could you want? I've had a few lovely, lazy days. You should try it. It will do you all the good in the world to take things easy for a while.' Sophie was enjoying herself. The look on Melissa's face was enough to stop a clock. She couldn't believe her ears.

'But how will I get to the airport? You can't leave me like this, Sophie. I won't allow it.' Melissa was red with fury.

'The rep will bring you to the airport. No worries.' Sophie chose to ignore her outburst. This only angered Melissa even more.

'But you're a nurse. You have a *duty* to sick people,' she raged. This wasn't the Sophie she knew. 'You can't leave me here on my own!'

'Watch me,' Sophie retorted as she

lifted her case from the bed. 'I just want to say before I go, you are the biggest cow going. You don't know how to be a friend. You use people. You drop them like hot potatoes when it suits. Well I've had enough of you, Melissa Harris. To be honest, I don't care if you have to walk back to London on your crutches. I couldn't give a hoot.'

She strode to the door. She was delighted to have told the other girl *exactly* what she thought of her. She turned and took one last look at her so-called friend.

'Goodbye Melissa. Enjoy the rest of your holiday. I know I'm going to enjoy mine. To tell you the truth, it's the *best* holiday I've ever had.'

Chapter Eight

Melissa stood at the window watching Sophie laughing with a man and a little girl. The man put her case into the boot of the BMW.

'What a bitch!' Melissa swore. Tears of rage wet her cheeks. How dare Sophie Mason talk to her the way she just had? The little jumped-up madam. Who did she think she was? She was just a boring, frumpy little dumpling. If it hadn't been for Melissa she'd have been stuck in London with no one to go on holidays with. And this was the thanks she got for her good deed!

The minute Melissa got back to London she was going to make a complaint to Sophie's bosses. She was going to say that Sophie wasn't fit to be a nurse. Imagine leaving a sick woman in dire straits. It was shocking.

Sophie would probably get the sack when the Matron heard about her cruelty. It would be good enough for her. And she was going to tell everyone at home what a selfish cow Sophie Mason was. Everyone thought she was such a nice goody-goody. Ha! Soon they'd know the truth. Melissa watched with slitted eyes as her former friend sat into the front of the BMW as if she owned it.

'What a nerve! What a hard-hearted slag,' she muttered as the big silver car sped out of the complex.

Melissa looked around the bedroom. Her heart sank. It was a

grotty little kip and she was stuck here for almost another week. What a horrific thought. Feeling very, very sorry for herself, Melissa sank onto the bed and cried bitterly.

★

'And this is your room, Sophie. I do hope you like it.' Elena, Juan's daughter, smiled as she showed Sophie her bedroom.

Sophie stared in delight at the bright, airy room that had its own balcony overlooking the sea.

'It's lovely, Mrs Suarez,' Sophie declared with pleasure.

'You must call me Elena,' the other woman insisted. 'You will become like one of the family.'

'I feel like one already,' Sophie laughed as Maria hugged her tightly. 'How about I bring this young lady to the beach and you can enjoy a little siesta?'

'That would be wonderful. The baby was kicking all night and I didn't get a wink of sleep. It must be a boy.' She patted her bump with pride.

'And I will make us the best paella ever for dinner, to celebrate your arrival,' Juan announced. He was delighted that everything was working out so well.

That night as Sophie lay in the big double bed looking out on a moon-lit sea she smiled happily. This was such a comfortable bed compared to the narrow, lumpy one she'd slept on since she'd arrived in Spain. Her *en suite* bathroom was spotless. It had been a pleasure to have a bath and wash the sand away after her afternoon on the beach.

Dinner had been delicious. Juan was

a marvellous cook. And she felt nicely tired after the two glasses of red wine Elena had pressed on her. 'You must have one for me.' Elena had laughed, sipping her soda water.

Later, Elena's brother had called by. His name was Carlos. He was a doctor. *And* he was drop-dead gorgeous.

Sophie blushed in the dark as she remembered a pair of smiling brown eyes twinkling at her attempts at Spanish.

'I will have to teach you,' he teased in English. She was very glad that Melissa was nowhere in sight.

For a moment she wondered what the other girl was doing. It had been one of the best moments in her life when she'd closed the door of the apartment. Guilt had not got the better of her. She hadn't been a doormat. For the first time in her life she had put herself first. It felt very good.

Sophie closed her eyes. She snuggled into the pillows and fell fast asleep as the moon shone silver on the sea and the stars sparkled like diamonds.

★

Melissa twisted and turned on her hard, narrow bed. Her leg itched inside the plaster cast and it was driving her mad. Needless to say there was no air-conditioning in her poky, little, kippy bedroom. She was afraid to open the sliding doors in case one of those awful little monsters got in. The insects were a nightmare.

How she hated Sophie Mason's guts, she thought grimly. She had spent the most boring time of her life lying on a lounger down by the pool. Four horrid kids had screamed and splashed in the pool for ages. The din had given her a headache. Later she had hobbled over to the bar and had a revolting burger and chips for her dinner. She'd tried to get pissed on *sangria*. It didn't help. She wasn't in the mood. She'd just got a headache for her trouble.

There wasn't even a sexy barman to flirt with, she thought mournfully. Pedro was fat and greasy. His shirt had tomato sauce on it. His nails were dirty. And he couldn't smile to save his life. She made a face in the dark. She hadn't even made an effort to be nice to him. Grumpy old sod.

This was the worst holiday she had ever been on and it was all Sophie Mason's fault. Tomorrow she was going to phone home and beg her mother to pay for a flight to get her home. She couldn't bear to stay in this hell-hole for another day.

Melissa slept fitfully. When she awoke, she sat up in bed glad that it was daylight. Her eye felt strange. She rubbed it. It was sore. She rooted in her bag and found her make-up case. A glance in her pocket-mirror caused her to squeal in dismay. Her eyelid had swollen to twice its normal size. It was red and watery and completely gruesome looking. One of those skanky little insects had bitten her. It was the last straw. Melissa found her mobile and dialled home.

'Mum, you have to send me money to get me home. It's a nightmare; Mum I'm all on my own. Sophie deserted me. I've got a broken leg and something terrible has happened to my eye. I think I'm going blind.' She wept.

'My poor darling! Of course I'll send you money. What happened? How did you break your leg? What do you mean Sophie's deserted you?' Rose Harris asked with concern.

'It's a long story,' Melissa sobbed.

'You'll never believe the way Sophie Mason treated me. She doesn't know how to be a friend. I'm never going to have anything to do with her again.'

Melissa poured her heart out to her mother who promised to organise a flight home that very day if possible.

Twelve hours later Melissa was on a flight to London. A handsome cabin attendant fussed over her and offered her a drink. Melissa sat back in her seat watching the lights of Spain twinkle beneath the plane. Thank God she was going home, she thought. It was a pity she couldn't really flirt with Mister Sexy, but she looked a sight with her swollen red eye and dirty foot peeking out from its plaster cast.

Regretfully she sipped her wine. It had been the worst holiday of her entire life. She was never going to speak to Sophie Mason again.

Chapter Nine

A year later ...

'Did you hear about Sophie Mason? She's engaged to some rich Spanish doctor. She met him when she was working in Majorca. They're getting married next month. I met her sister in a club last night. Sophie's flying the whole family out to Majorca for the wedding. Imagine! You never told me about the wedding. Are you going?' Ann Kelly asked Melissa as they tidied up the salon after a very busy day.

Melissa's fingers curled. Her lips tightened with envy. What a sly cow that Sophie Mason had turned out to be. She had left her alone in that grotty little apartment with a broken leg. And then she had gone and wangled her way into that Spanish family. It was galling to think that she had nabbed a rich Spanish doctor and was getting married! Melissa hadn't seen her from that day to this. And now to hear this shocking news. Was there no justice in the world?

'Don't mention that girl's name to me,' Melissa snapped. 'I thought she was a friend. Little did I know until she stabbed me in the back what a sly bitch she was.'

'She stabbed you in the back?' Angie was astonished.

'Don't be thick,' Melissa said crossly. 'I invited her to go on holidays and then she met these people and left me in the lurch on my own with a broken leg. Can you believe that?'

'*Really?* I'd never have thought it of Sophie. That's awful. I always thought she was very nice,' Ann remarked in surprise.

'Well she wasn't. She's as two-faced as they come. I don't want to talk about her,' Melissa declared with venom.

'Oh, OK. That's understandable. With friends like that who needs enemies?' Ann said quickly. 'Just as well you have me to go on holidays with this year.' She smiled. 'I wouldn't do anything like that. Not in a million years. You can depend on me.'

'I know, sweetie.' Melissa managed a smile. 'You'll love where we're going to. It has a marina full of yachts. There are loads of rich people hanging around in the cafés. It will be the best holiday ever.'

'I can't wait!' Ann said excitedly. 'Thanks for inviting me to come.'

'You're very welcome,' said Melissa kindly. 'Could you be a pet and finish off here? I've got a thumping headache.'

'Oh, OK,' Ann murmured. Funny how Melissa always got a thumping headache on Friday evenings when the salon had to be cleaned.

Melissa swanned out of the salon leaving her new best friend to tidy up. Ann would be an *excellent* holiday companion, she thought with satisfaction. Not like the soon-to-be-married two-faced Sophie.

★

A sunbeam danced through the stained-glass window just as Carlos placed the wedding ring on Sophie's finger. She smiled at him and felt as though her heart would burst with happiness. It was so hard to believe that she was standing beside him and the priest was blessing them as man and wife.

The past year had flown by. In fact, it was a year to the day that Melissa Harris had swanned off to Marbella and left her to holiday alone. What a difference a year makes. It had been the happiest year of her life.

She and Carlos had got on like a house on fire. He had a great sense of humour and delighted in teasing her. He had taught her Spanish. She could now speak it fluently. He'd shown her all around the beautiful island of Majorca, taking her to hidden beaches and whitewashed villages never seen by tourists. They'd fallen in love easily, with humour and affection. She had never felt more comfortable with anyone in her life.

She turned and smiled at her parents and sisters. It was wonderful to have them here. Juan and Elena had been so kind. She could hear Elena's baby boy cooing happily. He was a little angel. She couldn't wait to have a baby herself. Carlos loved children and they loved him. Maria was their flower girl. Sophie smiled at her husband and he smiled back. 'Hi, wife,' he whispered.

'Hi, husband,' she whispered back, squeezing his hand.

They kissed each other. It was the most perfect day of Sophie's life.

★

'What do you mean you're going up to Deya with that guy you met on Saturday?' Ann Kelly stared at Melissa in dismay.

'Oh sweetie, don't be like that. He's gorgeous. He's spending a fortune on me. Come on, I need to find a nice man after the rats I've been with,' she pouted.

'But you came on holidays with me. You *asked* me to come. What will I do by myself?'

'Look, I'm not your *nanny*,' Melissa said crossly. 'I'm going to Deya with Ramon and that's it. Deal with it.' She marched across the room, grabbed her case and walked out of the apartment.

Ann sat on her bed, stunned. Melissa had been a wagon from the moment they had come on holidays. It was clear she didn't care a bit about Ann or her holiday. Melissa wanted a man. She had gone all out to get one. She certainly wasn't going to let a so-called friend stand in the way.

Ann shook her head. It was starting to dawn on her that she had been used. Was this what had happened to Sophie Mason? Had Melissa treated her like dirt too? Most likely, Ann thought glumly.

It looked like she was on her own. She'd have to make the best of it. She packed her beach bag and headed for the sea.

Later, she strolled down to the marina. A wedding group passed by, car horns tooting and beeping. The bride looked radiant. Ann looked at her with a tinge of envy. Her eyes widened. It was Sophie Mason. Today was Sophie's wedding day. What a coincidence. It was a pity Melissa couldn't see her. What a kick in the ass that would be for the skanky slapper.

At least Sophie had had a happy ending, surrounded by family and friends. It was more than Melissa Harris would ever have. She didn't know the meaning of the word 'friend'. That would be her loss in life.

Look at how Sophie Mason's life had changed after coming on holiday with Melissa Harris. Sophie had been in the same boat as she was. Something good might happen to her too, Ann thought excitedly. Feeling happier, she joined in the cheers of the onlookers as Sophie and her husband drove past waving.